A bridge
is a poem
and is only there
for you to cross.

Otters, Snails and Tadpole Tails

Poems from the Wetlands

By Eric Ode

Illustrated by Ruth Harper

Kane Miller
A DIVISION OF EDC PUBLISHING

WILL I FIND YOU HERE?

Will I find you here
where cedar wears her mossy shawl,
where herons soar and blackbirds call,
where otters splash and crayfish crawl
among the reeds?

Where spider's silken web is spun,
where mayflies flit and rivers run,
where goslings follow one-by-one
as mother leads?

Where raccoons roam and weasels creep,
where cattails wave and willows weep,
where muskrats vanish, diving deep,
then reappear?

Will I find you here?

THE SALAMANDER

The salamander and her kin
sneak about in slimy skin,
and as for status, live within
the family amphibian,
which simply means, so I've been told,
their skin is wet; their blood is cold.
And further, if I understand,
their home is both on pond and land,
which, I declare, seems rather grand!
And though there may be creatures grander,
let me simply say with candor,
I adore the salamander.

THE FROG

Lily pad leaper,
moss carpet creeper,
swimmer in slippery skin;
pond water wader,
heron evader,
slickered from flippers to chin.

Web-footed tracker,
caddisfly snacker,
wholly at home on the bog;
splash-happy springer,
star-shadow singer,
lullaby bringer,
the frog.

FIDDLEHEAD

Nimble little fiddlehead,
nuzzled in a fuzzy hug.
Dreamer in a mossy bed,
curled and cuddled, soft and snug.

Stretch and catch a sunny spark
here where other leaves are basking.
Sleepy little question mark,
how I wonder what you're asking.

THE SNAIL

A helmet home
upon her back,
a head,
a tail,
a silvery track.
A single foot
to scoot along,
without a whispered word
or song.

Turn the leaf
and trace the trail
to find her there,
a silent snail.

CATTAIL

What a strange and silly cat
to make yourself at home like that
with no concern for rain or flood;
your tender paws in sticky mud.

What fussy pussy cat would dare
to stroll the marsh and settle there
and never hiss or spit or stir
while on your tail
a blackbird sits
and nips and nibbles at your fur?

THE HERON

The heron measures the morning
in slow, perfect strides
until, at last,
she gathers the patterns
beneath her wide, steel wings
and rises,
slicing the sky
like scissors
through faded denim.

THE BEAVER

Speak
with the beaver,
if he'll dare spare
the time. Ask about his
home of steeply heaped limbs;
a home that first seems built with
the carelessness of laundry piled upon
an unmade bed. Speak with the beaver.
He will tell you instead of how each bite felt
against his teeth and tongue. He'll talk of the taste,
the smell, the delicious muddy thud of each tree as it finally fell.

DRAGONFLY

The weary knight
climbs from the water
and sheds his armor
to take flight
as the dragon.

THE DIVING BEETLE

Diving beetle, do you wish
to be instead a frog or fish?
Such different worlds you seem to straddle.
Here you plunge. You puddle-paddle,
only later taking flight
the way a proper beetle might.

You're clearly bug in shape and size
with beetle legs and wings and eyes.
But, little beetle, what's the meaning?
Why this need for submarining?
Do you wonder, do you wish
to be instead a frog or fish?

THE WATER STRIDER

One bug flies.
One crawls,
one swims.
The water strider
glides and skims;
rides atop
the pond or brook.

Small and silent.
Lightning quick.
An easy bug
to overlook.
But sinkable?
Unthinkable!

THE RIVER OTTER

The river otter
twists and tosses,
loops and spins,
out and in.
He turns and totters,
twirls until
we can not tell
where one end ends
and one begins.

We wonder as
we watch him roll
and jumble–tumble
over, under,
through the water—
how does he keep
from tying into
one big otter knot
while behaving
quite exactly
as a river otter
ought?

THE DUCK

The duck
does not complain
of summer showers.
He never cowers
at the rain
or finds a need
to be upset
at being wet.

While others hide,
he glides about,
considering the pitter
and patter
splattering
his feathered head
as blessing
and luck.
Why should such weather matter
to a duck?

THE GARTER SNAKE

From here,
    she first appears
as a small, black pool
        poured near
    the trail's edge
until
    one step too heavy
        sends her slipping
    unheard
between the slender fingers
    of sedges and reeds.
So easily she turns
    from serpent to stream,
        coil to oil.

THE RACCOON

When I watch him nab
a darting fish,
a crawling crab,
a scaly snake,
a fuzzy vole,
an earthworm from
its grimy hole,

When I watch him snatch
the berries from
a thorny patch,
a beetle from
its leafy bed,
a spider from
her silky thread,

When I watch him pluck
a crawdad from
the mud and muck,
a hidden clutch
of nested eggs,
a bullfrog by
its chubby legs,

It's then I know,
if you should ask,
why Raccoon wears
his bandit mask.

THE TURTLE

In the water,
the turtle seems
a capsized boat;
unconcerned
at being
upturned,
all four oars
still rowing.

SALMON

They crowd the river,
moving with
tail-kicked flashes,
flicks,
and splashes,
like a battered
and proud
parade,
their red banners
streaming,

worn,
tattered,
and frayed.
They are
a funeral procession
marching
in memory
of themselves.

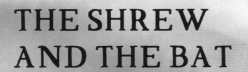

THE SHREW
AND THE BAT

"A riddle," said the shrew
to the little brown bat.
"Who flits about, this way and that,
to snatch a mayfly, moth, or gnat?
While I am found upon the ground
but wish I might be heaven-bound,
who climbs the sky on satin wings,
collecting songs the starlight sings?
Who chases through those spaces
where I only dream to go?
Do you know, little bat?
Do you know?"

"I'll answer that,"
replied the bat.
"But first, my little shrew,
here's a riddle just for you.

"Who wears a narrow, whiskered nose?
Who knows the joys of muddy toes?
Who prowls the marshy floor and feeds
on spiders, slugs, and centipedes?
Who dances through the tender reeds,
and skips and skitters, slips and weaves
beneath a bed of littered leaves,
in and out,
to and fro,
where I could never go?
Think of that,"
said the bat.
"Think of that."

To everyone who finds beauty and poetry in healthy wetland ecosystems.
Maybe that's you! – EO

These pictures were made possible by the Superpowers of
my hero hubby, Russ – RH

First Edition 2019
Kane Miller, A Division of EDC Publishing

Text copyright © Eric Ode, 2019
Illustrations copyright © Ruth Harper, 2019

For information contact:
Kane Miller, A Division of EDC Publishing
www.kanemiller.com
www.edcpub.com
www.usbornebooksandmore.com

Library of Congress Control Number: 2018942375

Manufactured by Regent Publishing Services, Hong Kong
Printed November 2018 in ShenZhen, Guangdong, China
1 2 3 4 5 6 7 8 9 10

ISBN: 978-1-61067-747-9